THE SUPER SPREADER

Maria Giordano - Text
Marc Hendrickx - Drawings

Connor Court Publishing

Published in 2020 by Connor Court Publishing Pty Ltd

Connor Court Publishing Pty Ltd
PO Box 7257
Redland Bay QLD 4165
sales@connorcourt.com
www.connorcourt.com
Phone 0497-900-685

Printed in Australia

ISBN: 9781922449290

THIS BOOK BELONGS TO

_____

Where is the Super Spreader?

Is he at the Hotel?

Is he at the protest?

Is he at the meatworks?

No!

So, where is he?

He is at Church!

suffering
4
all of us

He is with you at the wedding.

He is waiting for you at home!

At your family dinner table!

He is at the Golf Course.

And he is definitely with you when you decide to sit down at a park bench.

Thankfully, he keeps away from the Supermarket.

And the bottle shop?

No, the Super Spreader would rather eat a souvlaki?

www.ingramcontent.com/pod-product-compliance
Lightning Source LLC
Chambersburg PA
CBHW041641010726
47507CB00011B/425